ATOS BL: 6.3
PTS: 0.5
NF

The Colony of Rhode Island

A Primary Source History

Jake Miller

The Rosen Publishing Group's

PowerKids Press™

New York

Published in 2006 by The Rosen Publishing Group, Inc.
29 East 21st Street, New York, NY 10010

First Edition

Editor: Jennifer Way
Book Design: Ginny Chu
Photo Researcher: Cindy Reiman

Photo credits: Cover © SuperStock, Inc.; p. 4 National Archives, The Hague: 4.VEL inventory number 520; p. 4 (inset) Scala/Art Resource, NY; pp. 6, 8 The New York Public Library/Art Resource, NY; pp. 6 (inset), 16 (inset) © Getty Images; p. 8 (inset) State of Rhode Island and Providence Plantations, Office of the Secretary of State/State Archives Division; p. 9 Jack Boucher, photographer, HABS, RI, 3-NEWP, 29-4, Library of Congress Prints and Photographs Division; p. 10 Courtesy of Haffenreffer Musuem of Anthropology, Brown University; pp. 10 (inset), 16, 20 (inset) Mary Evans Picture Library; p. 12 Emmet Collection, Miriam and Ira D. Wallach Division of Art, Prints and Photographs, The New York Public Library, Astor, Lenox and Tilden Foundations; p. 12 (inset) Smithsonian Institution, Washington DC, USA/Bridgeman Art Library; p. 14 Private Collection, Phillips, Fine Art Auctioneers, New York, USA/ Bridgeman Art Library; p. 14 (inset) Library of Congress Prints and Photographs Division; p. 18 © Delaware Art Museum, Wilmington, USA, Howard Pyle Collection/Bridgeman Art Library; p. 18 (inset) National Portrait Gallery, Smithsonian Institution/ Art Resource, NY; p. 20 Picture Collection, The Branch Libraries, The New York Public Library, Astor, Lenox and Tilden Foundations.

Library of Congress Cataloging-in-Publication Data

Miller, Jake, 1969–
    The colony of Rhode Island : a primary source history / Jake Miller.— 1st ed.
        p. cm. — (The primary source library of the thirteen colonies and the Lost Colony)
    Includes index.
    ISBN 1-4042-3032-7 (library binding)
    1. Rhode Island—History—Colonial period, ca. 1600–1775—Juvenile literature. 2. Rhode Island—History—1775–1865—Juvenile literature. I. Title.
    F82.M646 2006
    974.5'02—dc22
                                                2004027048

Manufactured in the United States of America

Contents

Adriaen Block created this map around 1614. It includes parts of today's Rhode Island. Block established trade with Native Americans on this trip. This led to other Dutch people coming to the area to trade. Inset: On his trip to North America, Giovanni da Verrazano met Wampanoag Native Americans, who helped him sail up the Narragansett Bay.

Exploring Narragansett Bay

Rhode Island is located in New England. It is bordered by Massachusetts to the north and the east and by Connecticut to the west. The state consists of several islands and the land on Narragansett Bay. The first recorded European to see the area was the Italian explorer Giovanni da Verrazano. He sailed into Narragansett Bay in 1524. The place where he landed is now the city of Newport. At the time there were many Native Americans living there, including the Narragansett and the Wampanoag peoples.

After Verrazano no Europeans came to the area until 1614. Then the Dutch sailor Adriaen Block explored one of the islands, which was later named Block Island for him. Soon after many Dutch visited the area to trade with the Native Americans.

From A Key into the Language of America

"An help to the Language of the Natives in that part of America called New-England. Together, with briefe observations of the Customes, Manners and Worships, etc. of the aforesaid Natives . . ."

This passage from the title page of Roger Williams' 1643 book says it will explain the language and society of the Native Americans of New England. These explanations came from Williams' own observations.

Roger Williams left the Massachusetts Bay Colony so that he could follow his religious beliefs. Religious freedom played an important part in the formation of the Rhode Island Colony. Williams is shown here meeting the Narragansett. Inset: This is the title page of Williams' A Key into the Language of America.

Early English Settlers

In the 1620s, colonists from England began to settle along the coast in New England. They founded the Plymouth Colony and the Massachusetts Bay Colony in today's Massachusetts. The first English settler came to Rhode Island in 1635. William Blackstone left Boston, in the Massachusetts Bay Colony, to build a farm in Rhode Island.

Roger Williams was another early settler. Williams was forced to leave the Massachusetts Bay Colony for questioning its laws. In 1636, Williams and a group of his followers settled on Narragansett Bay. Williams named the town Providence, which means "God's guidance," because he felt that God had guided him to start this new town. Their settlement was the first English town in what would later become Rhode Island.

In 1644, Roger Williams brought back the Patent for Providence Plantations. It took until
1647 for the four settlements to reach an agreement to join together under this patent. The
settlements were Portsmouth, Newport, Warwick, and Providence. Inset: Rhode Island
received its charter in 1663.

Settling Rhode Island

Other religious **nonconformists** soon came to Rhode Island. In 1638, John Clarke, William Coddington, and William and Anne Hutchinson founded Portsmouth. Although these settlers had bought their land from the Native Americans, the Massachusetts colonies wanted to take over these lands.

In 1644, Roger Williams got a **patent** from England's **Parliament**. This protected the settlements from being taken over by the Massachusetts colonies. The settlements joined under the patent in 1647 and named the colony Rhode Island and the Providence **Plantations**.

People who belonged to religions other than that of the established church, such as Quakers, Jews, and French Protestants, were not welcome in many places in the 1600s. Roger Williams welcomed these people to settle in Rhode Island. Touro Synagogue in Newport, shown above, is the oldest existing Jewish temple in America. It opened in 1762.

This picture shows colonists fighting King Philip's War. Inset: Metacomet, known as King Philip to the New England settlers, was a Wampanoag leader. He began a war against the Plymouth Colony in Massachusetts because the Wampanoag were angry about losing their lands to the colonists.

King Philip's War

Rhode Island's early settlers had good relationships with their Native American neighbors. The settlers in Massachusetts did not get along with the nearby Native Americans, and the fighting between the two groups spilled over into Rhode Island.

In 1675, a Wampanoag chief named Metacomet, known as King Philip to the settlers, led a war against the Plymouth Colony. This became known as King Philip's War. Rhode Island did not join the other colonies in this war, but it had an effect on them.

In December 1675, a group of Massachusetts colonists burned down a Narragansett village in Rhode Island, killing 600 people. The next spring the Narragansett attacked Providence and other Rhode Island settlements. King Philip was killed in August 1676, which led to the Native Americans' loss and ended the war.

During the eighteenth century, Newport became an important center of businesses such as shipbuilding and trade. Inset: Colonists in Rhode Island built mills throughout the eighteenth century. The mills, like this one in Pawtucket, helped to build Rhode Island's wealth.

Rhode Island's Wealth

Many of the people who settled in Rhode Island came to make money. The mainland had rich farmland. Rhode Island's coast was home to fishing and shipbuilding businesses. Coastal towns such as Newport were busy centers of trade. By the mid-1700s, Providence began to top Newport as the commercial and political center of the colony.

Rhode Island gained more land in the eighteenth century. A 1727 land disagreement with Connecticut was settled in Rhode Island's favor. In 1747, an agreement with Massachusetts also added land to the colony. Adding land to Rhode Island helped the colony to grow both in size and in wealth. During this time Rhode Island also experienced the leadership of Samuel Cranston. The city of Cranston, Rhode Island, is named for him.

From By the King, A Proclamation (1762)

"And whereas for the putting an end to the Calamities of War, as soon and as far as may be possible, it has been agreed between Us, His Most Christian Majesty, and His Catholick Majesty, as follows; that is to say,

That as soon as the Preliminaries shall be signed and ratified, all Hostilities should cease at Sea and at Land."

The above passage states that the king of Great Britain wishes for fighting between France and Britain to stop. The proclamation goes on to say that the signing of a treaty by both sides will bring an official end to the French and Indian War.

The French and Indian War lasted from 1754 to 1763. The war was fought over the land west of the 13 colonies. It was an expensive war for Britain, and the colonies were expected to help pay for it through taxes. Inset: This 1762 royal proclamation ended the fighting of the French and Indian War.

Britain's Unfair Taxes

Rhode Island was the most independent of the 13 colonies. The colony's 1763 **charter** allowed the colonists to elect their governor and to make their own laws. This changed after the British beat the French in the **French and Indian War**. The British decided that the colonies should help pay for the war by paying higher taxes. In 1764, Parliament passed a tax on molasses called the Sugar Act. The colonists did not think it was fair that a parliament that they had not elected was passing these taxes.

The Rhode Island colonists disobeyed these new laws. They brought molasses into the colony illegally to avoid paying the tax. They attacked tax collectors' ships and burned them. Rhode Island presented some of the strongest opposition to Britain of any of the colonies.

THE

RIGHTS

OF

COLONIES

EXAMINED.

Stephen Hopkins

PUBLISHED BY AUTHORITY.

*PROVIDENCE:
PRINTED BY *WILLIAM GODDARD.*
M.DCC.LXV.*

In 1772, Rhode Island colonists burned the British ship Gaspée when it ran aground in the Narragansett Bay. Inset: Stephen Hopkins, the chief judge of Rhode Island, wrote The Rights of Colonies Examined in 1765 to protest the Stamp Act.

Rhode Island Protests

Rhode Island colonists opposed unfair laws as well as unfair taxes. Many Rhode Islanders joined a group called the **Sons of Liberty** to **protest** the Stamp Act of 1765, a tax on anything made of paper. Strong protests throughout the colonies led to the end of this tax the following year. **Smugglers** in Rhode Island did not openly disobey these unfair taxes. Instead they sneaked their goods past the tax collectors. In 1772, the British sent a ship called the *Gaspée* to stop smugglers in the Narragansett Bay. On June 9, 1772, the *Gaspée* ran aground while it was chasing a smuggler. A group of colonists sailed out to the boat, took it by force, and burned it down. This act is often seen as the first assault by the colonies against Britain in the period leading up to the **American Revolution**.

This painting shows Nathanael Greene taking over the command of the southern Continental army from Horatio Gates in 1780. Inset: Greene, of Warwick, Rhode Island, was second in command of the army. He led troops in the South during the American Revolution.

Declaring Independence

The British were angry that the colonists were resisting their laws. In 1774, Parliament passed four laws called the Coercive Acts. These laws were meant to punish the colonies for protesting British laws. These laws made their relations worse.

On May 17, 1774, the leaders in Providence called for a Continental Congress, which would bring the colonies together to fight the British. The First Continental Congress met on September 5, 1774, in Philadelphia, Pennsylvania. Stephen Hopkins and Samuel Ward **represented** Rhode Island. The American Revolution began on April 19, 1775. On May 4, 1776, Rhode Island was the first colony to announce its independence from Britain. Two months later the Second Continental Congress signed the **Declaration of Independence**.

Although the Battle of Rhode Island had no clear winner, it was viewed as an example of the colonists' bravery. This picture appeared in a magazine soon after the battle. Inset: Colonel John Sullivan and his Rhode Island troops guarded Newport in the Battle of Rhode Island, but the British forced them to go back to Providence.

The American Revolution in Rhode Island

Rhode Island's ships, soldiers, and money helped the colonies fight for independence. Rhode Island men were important leaders in the war. Esak Hopkins of Providence was the first commander in chief of the Continental navy. General Nathanael Greene was second in command of the Continental army.

British forces occupied Newport in December 1776. In August 1778, Colonel John Sullivan from Rhode Island led troops against the British, but the British held off the attack. This was known as the Battle of Rhode Island. The British left Newport in 1779. The Continental navy could then send ships from this port to attack the British forces in Virginia. In 1781, the Continental army won the Battle of Yorktown, in Virginia. This win brought an end to the fighting.

The Struggle to Form a New Nation

After the war officially ended in 1783 with the Treaty of Paris, the former colonies had to find a way to work together as a nation. During the war the colonies followed the **Articles of Confederation**. The articles treated each state more like its own country than as a part of a single country.

Rhode Islanders preferred this weak central government. When the Constitutional Convention was called in 1787, Rhode Island did not send any representatives. The other 12 states passed a new **constitution** in September 1787. The creation of the **Bill of Rights** assured Rhode Islanders that their freedoms would be protected. On May 29, 1790, Rhode Island approved the Constitution and joined the United States as the thirteenth state.

Glossary

American Revolution (uh-MER-uh-ken reh-vuh-LOO-shun) Battles that soldiers from the colonies fought against Britain for freedom, from 1775 to 1783.

Articles of Confederation (AR-tih-kulz UV kun-feh-deh-RAY-shun) The laws that governed the United States before the Constitution was created.

Bill of Rights (BIL UV RYTS) The part of the U.S. Constitution that explains the rights of citizens.

charter (CHAR-tur) An official agreement giving someone permission to do something.

constitution (kon-stuh-TOO-shun) The basic rules by which a country or state are governed.

Declaration of Independence (deh-kluh-RAY-shun UV in-duh-PEN-dints) A paper signed July 4, 1776, announcing that the American colonies were free from British rule.

French and Indian War (FRENCH AND IN-dee-un WOR) The battles fought between 1754 and 1763 by England, France, and Native Americans for control of North America.

nonconformists (non-kun-FOR-mists) People who act or believe differently than most people.

Parliament (PAR-leh-ment) The group in England that makes that country's laws.

patent (PA-tent) A document that gives someone claim to an area of land.

plantations (plan-TAY-shunz) Very large farms where crops are grown.

protest (PROH-test) To act out in disagreement.

represented (reh-prih-ZENT-ed) Stood for.

smugglers (SMUH-glurz) People who sneak things in and out of a country.

Sons of Liberty (SUNZ UV LIH-ber-tee) Groups of American colonists who protested the British government's taxes and unfair treatment before the American Revolution.

Index

Primary Sources

Page 4. Map of the East Coast of North America (detail). 1614, Adriaen Block. **Page 4. Inset.** *Giovanni da Verrazano* (detail). Painting, 16th Century, Anonymous, Galleria Comunale, Prato, Italy. **Page 6. Inset.** *A Key into the Language of America* (title page). 1643, Roger Williams, Rosenbach Museum & Library, Philadelphia, PA. **Page 8. Inset.** *Charter of Rhode Island and Providence Plantations* (detail). 1663, Library of Congress, Washington, D.C. **Page 12.** Southwest view of Newport. 1783, New York Public Library. **Page 12. Inset.** The first cotton mill in America, established by Samuel Slater at Pawtucket, Rhode Island. Oil-on-canvas painting, circa 18th century, American School, Smithsonian Institution, Washington, D.C. **Page 14.** *The Death of General Wolfe.* Oil-on-panel painting, 1771, Benjamin West, private collection. **Page 14. Inset.** *By the King, a Proclamation* (detail). 1763, Library of Congress Prints and Photographs Division, Washington, D.C. **Page 16. Inset.** *The Rights of Colonies Examined* (title page). 1765, Stephen Hopkins, Hulton Archive. **Page 18. Inset.** *Nathanael Greene.* Pewter medal, circa 1781, Augustin Dupre, National Portrait Gallery, Smithsonian Institution, Washington, D.C. **Page 20.** *Scene of engagement on Rhode Island, Aug. 29, 1778* (Battle of Rhode Island). 1778, New York Public Library.

Web Sites

Due to the changing nature of Internet links, PowerKids Press has developed an online list of Web sites related to the subject of this book. This site is updated regularly. Please use this link to access the list:
www.powerkidslinks.com/pstclc/rhodeisl/